DOC 2 DOC: TONY AND JACE LEARN ABOUT THE HEART

©2019 by Dale Okorodudu

Published by BMWC Media, Dallas, Texas

Dear Parents & Teachers,

I'm so excited that you're reading this book to your children. I think it's important for parents & educators to engage our youth in the sciences from an early age. The simple act of you flipping these pages for a child is doing just that.

I've purposely made this series a little challenging for the listed age range. One thing I've learned is that we should never underestimate our kids' potential. More often than not, they'll surprise us with their smarts.

As you read this book with your children, be sure to remind them it is fictional. At times, the characters will do things that children should not do on their own in real life. When there is a real medical situation, all children should contact a trusted adult immediately, and in emergency situations, call 911.

One last thing! We've got a special treat for you and your kid. Be sure to visit www.DoctorDaleMD.com/D2D-Heart. Thanks for exposing the kiddos to the field of science and medicine!

Praying for many blessings to you and your kiddos!

Dr. Dale

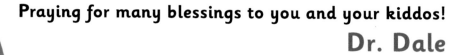

This book is dedicated to Mavyn. I love you Babygirl!

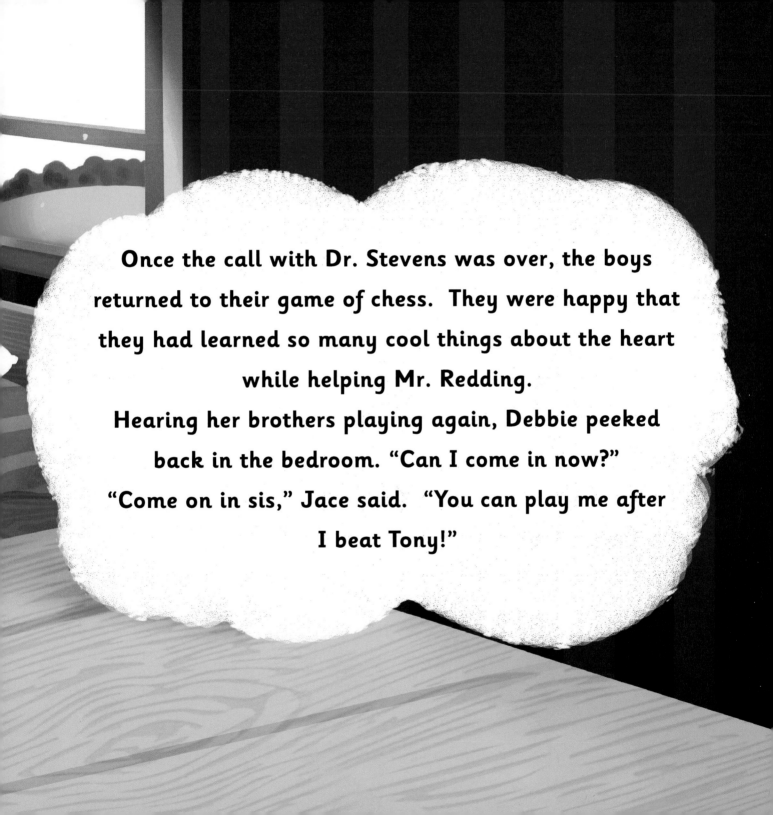

Once the call with Dr. Stevens was over, the boys returned to their game of chess. They were happy that they had learned so many cool things about the heart while helping Mr. Redding.

Hearing her brothers playing again, Debbie peeked back in the bedroom. "Can I come in now?"

"Come on in sis," Jace said. "You can play me after I beat Tony!"

At dinner that night, Tony and Jace told their parents about everything they learned while helping Mr. Redding.

"Great job, guys," said mom. "We're so proud of you. Mr. Redding was very happy that you helped refer him to a cardiologist. He's going to do great!"

Dad nodded his head in agreement. "You guys did excellent! But remember to keep studying so you can learn about the other parts of the body. There will be a lot more people for you to help."

Debbie's Quiz

Hi friends! Did you like the story? Let's see if you remember what we learned.

- Where is your heart? Can you point to it?
- Why do we need a heart?
- What is another name for a heart doctor?
- What protects your heart from being injured?
- How many chambers are in your heart?

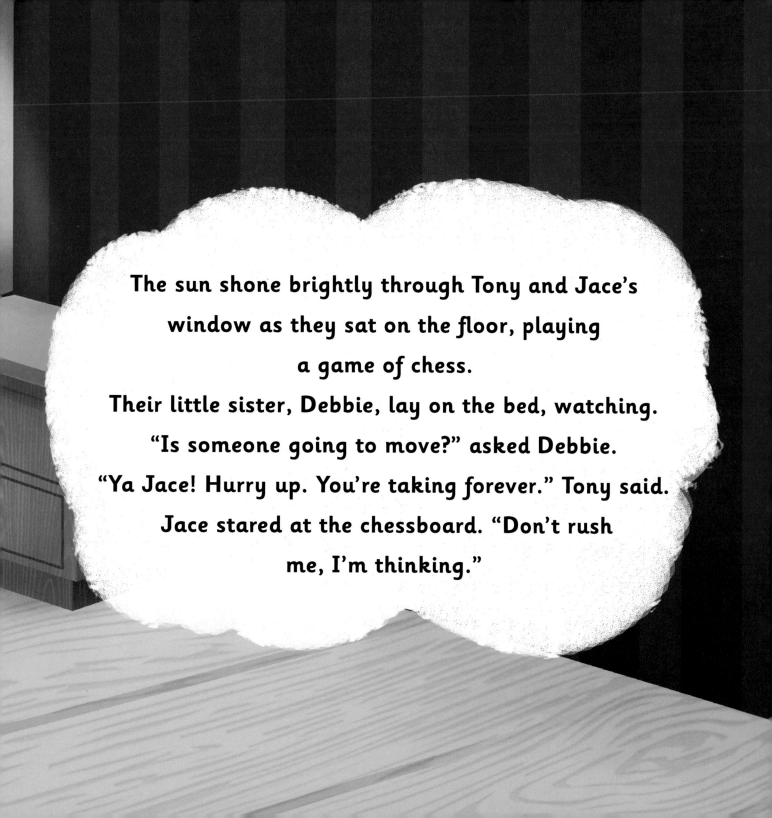

The sun shone brightly through Tony and Jace's
window as they sat on the floor, playing
a game of chess.
Their little sister, Debbie, lay on the bed, watching.
"Is someone going to move?" asked Debbie.
"Ya Jace! Hurry up. You're taking forever." Tony said.
Jace stared at the chessboard. "Don't rush
me, I'm thinking."

Just when Jace was about to make his move, Tony's tablet made a dinging noise that sounded like a doorbell. He recognized the sound; Mom was calling them on video. He jumped up, ran over and tapped the screen to answer the video call. His mom appeared with a big smile on her face and wearing her white coat.

"Hi mom!"

"Hi son! I've got a cool patient here. Do you and Jace want to help me take care of him?"

Tony's eyes lit up. "Of course!"

Mom smiled. "Great, I'm sending you his information now. Oh, and remember to let your sister know that when she gets a little older, she can start helping too."

"Okay mom, we'll tell her." Tony ended the call then turned to his brother, "Jace we have to finish the game later. Mom needs our help."

Jace looked at his sister, "You heard what he said Debbie. We've got work to do. Go play somewhere else."

"But, I wanna play doctor too..." said Debbie.

"You're not old enough yet. This is serious business. We can play later." Jace pointed to the door as he shooed her away.

Tony and Jace loved helping people and wanted to be doctors like their parents. They enjoyed learning about all the awesome parts of the body and were always excited when their mom called them about a patient.

"It's Mr. Redding," Tony said while studying his tablet. "He's worried he might have heart problems, and he's having some strange symptoms right now."

"Symp-what?" Jace asked scratching his chin.

"Symptom," said Tony. "It's a sign that something might be wrong with his body."

Tony smiled. He knew exactly what to do. Mom and dad always taught them that if they needed help, they could call special types of doctors for different parts of the body.

Tony looked at Jace. "I'm going to call Dr. Stevens. He can help us. He's a cardiologist."

"A cardio-what?" asked Jace.

"A cardiologist," said Tony. "That means he's a doctor who takes care of people's hearts."

Tony tapped his tablet screen to start the video
call, then waited a few moments.

"Dr. Stevens here!" said a warm, kind voice.
Dr. Stevens had graying hair, square glasses, and a
friendly smile. "Ah, Tony and Jace, what's going on?"

Tony explained Mr. Redding's problems while
Jace emailed Mr. Redding's medical history to
Dr. Stevens for review.

"Ok, I understand now," said Dr. Stevens.

"Boys, let's review a few things first. Do you know where your heart is?"

"Yep, that's easy," Jace said as he pointed to his left chest. "It's over here."

Dr. Stevens smiled. "Brilliant Jace! You're right. Now let's see what it really looks like."

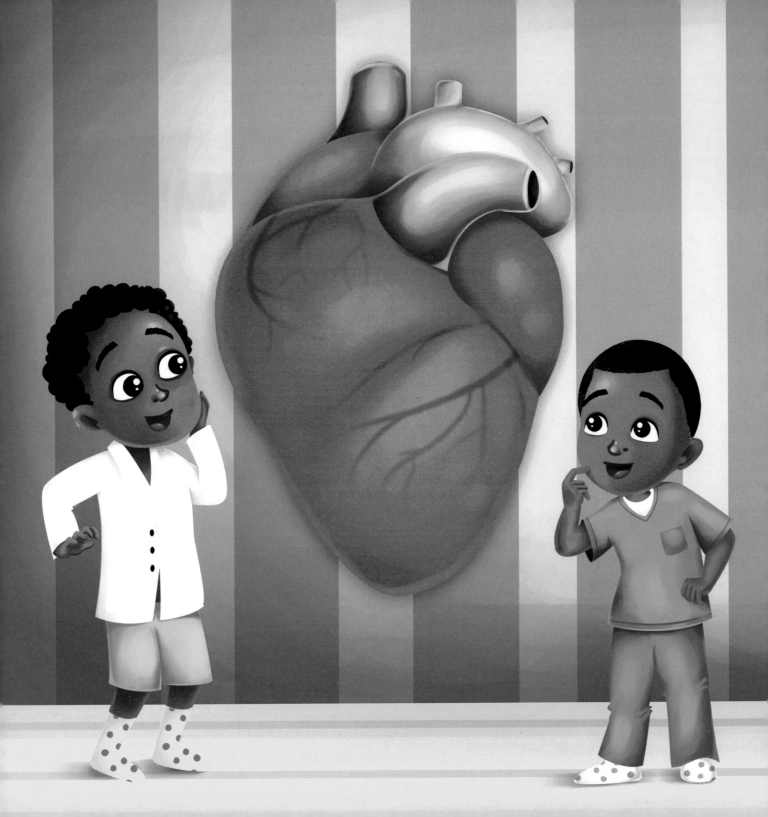

Suddenly, a colorful image of the human heart popped up as Dr. Stevens continued teaching. "The heart is very important. It pumps blood through the body."

"But why do we need blood?" asked Jace.

Dr. Stevens said, "Blood carries oxygen and nutrients to all the different parts of your body. Just think about it, right now your heart is pumping blood to your brain, kidneys, and lungs. If they don't get oxygen, they'll stop working."

"I definitely need a lot of oxygen," Tony grinningly said. "I want my body to keep on working right!"

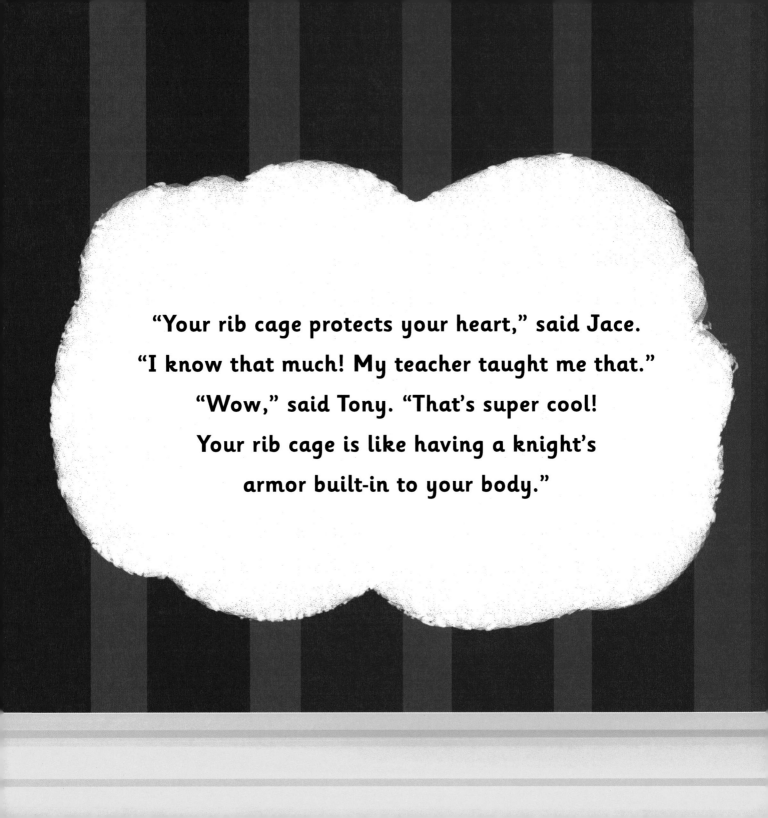

"Your rib cage protects your heart," said Jace.
"I know that much! My teacher taught me that."
"Wow," said Tony. "That's super cool!
Your rib cage is like having a knight's
armor built-in to your body."

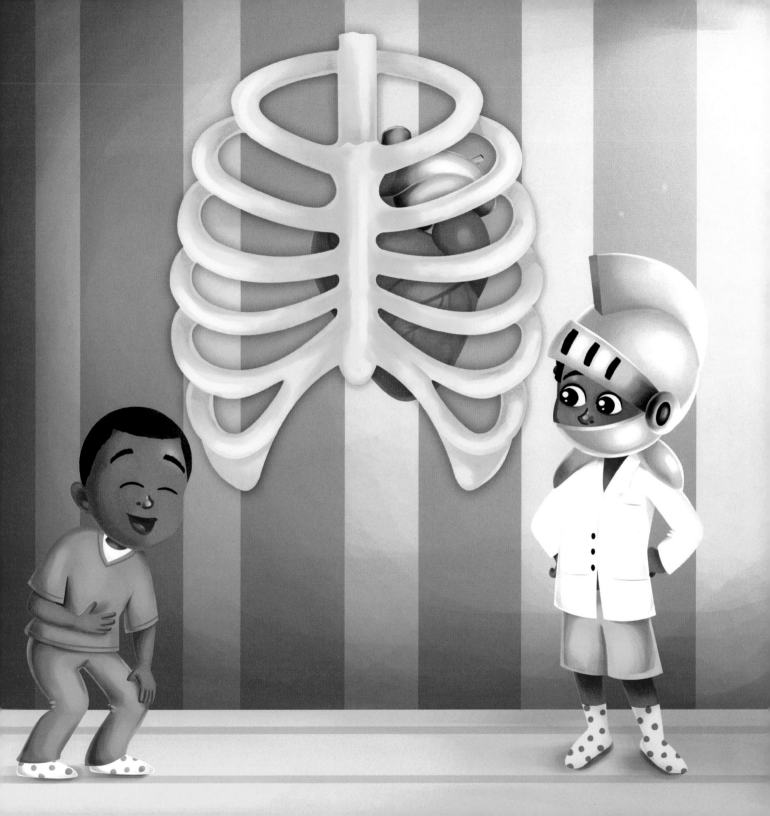

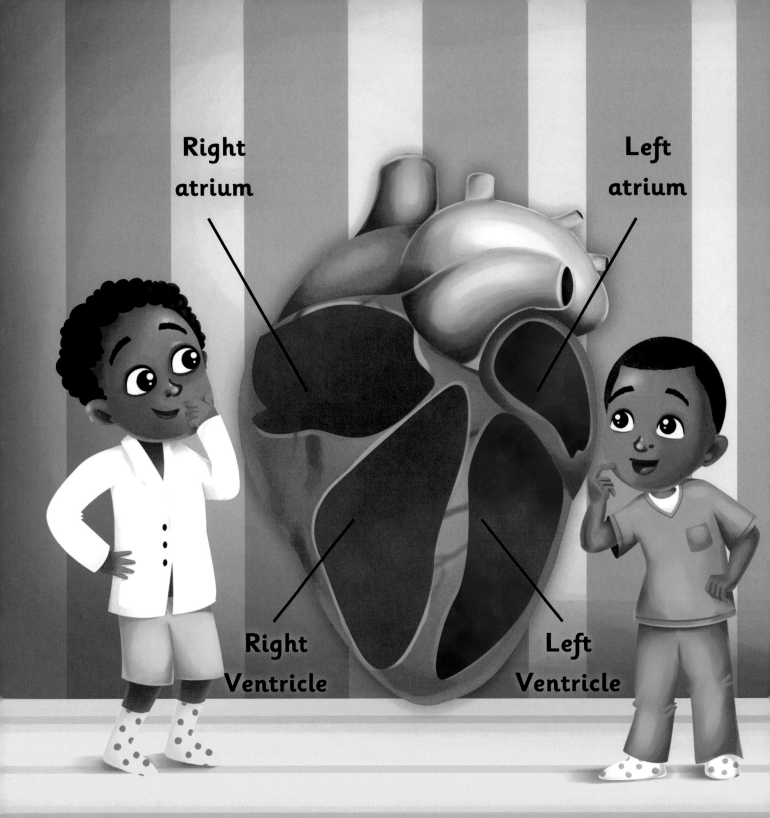

"Very true," said Dr. Stevens. "Let's take a closer look at the heart. It has four chambers: the left atrium, right atrium, left ventricle, and right ventricle. The blood has to go through all of them to get to the rest of the body."

"Awesome!" said Jace.

Tony tapped the screen again, and another picture of a heart appeared. This time, the boys could see the inside of it.

"There are also four valves!" Dr. Stevens continued. "See? These valves make sure that blood goes only one way. We don't want blood going backward do we boys?"

"No sir!" Jace said. "Our body is like a really cool machine."

"Dr. Stevens..." Tony said. "What do you think
is the coolest thing about the heart?"

"Now, that's a hard question," said Dr. Stevens, "There
are so many awesome things."

Jace threw up his hand to stop Dr. Stevens and
get his attention. "You have to pick one!"

"Okay, here's my favorite. Your heart beats about
100,000 times a day. Can you believe that?"

"Whoaaaa!" Tony looked surprised. "I can't even
count to 100,000. That's a lot!"

Dr. Stevens laughed. "Back to business boys. Tell me more about your patient."

"Okay," said Tony as he continued to explain the rest of Mr. Redding's symptoms.

"What do you think, junior docs?" asked Dr. Stevens.

"I think Mr. Redding needs to see a cardiologist like you," Jace said with a proud smile. "That's a doctor that takes care of hearts."

Dr. Stevens nodded. "I think you're right, Jace! Send him my way and I'll help take care of him."

"I'm referring him to you right away, doctor!" said Tony.

"I'll see him today," Dr. Stevens replied. "And make sure that Mr. Redding knows to call 911 if he has an emergency."

Jace waved goodbye. "Will do doc."